TALES OF THE SUPERNATURAL

Wizards and Sorcerers

TALES OF THE SUPERNATURAL

Wizards and Sorcerers
by David Oakden

ROURKE PUBLICATIONS, INC.
Windermere, Florida 32786

Library of Congress Cataloging in Publication Data

Oakden, David, 1947-
  Wizards & sorcerers.

  (Tales of the supernatural)
  Summary: Five tales of wizardry from Asia,
Africa, and Europe.
  1. Fairy tales. [1. Fairy tales. 2. Witch-
craft—Fiction. 3. Folklore] I. Title.
II. Title: Wizards and sorcerers. III. Series.
PZ7.01017Wj 1982   398.2'2   82-10226
ISBN 0-86625-206-1

CONTENTS

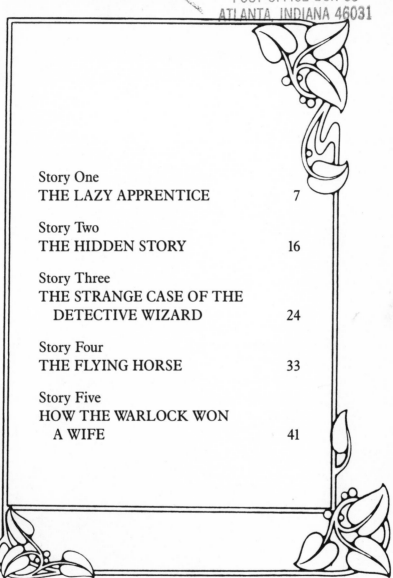

A collection of enchantments, bewitchings and strange happenings. These stories are in turn haunting, funny and enthralling.

Story One

The Lazy Apprentice

In the pot something was bubbling. Purple and yellow wreaths of steam coiled and curled over the iron rim and on to the cobbled floor. The smell was terrible.

"Master! Master!" called a boy who had been given the job of watching the pot. He was small for his age and his face was smudged with soot. He wiped more soot on to it from his scruffy sleeve and called again in a frightened voice, "Master! The pot! It's on fire!"

A tall, stooping figure appeared in a doorway at the top of a flight of steps. He was dressed in a long black cloak which almost covered his velvet slippers, and on top of his long white hair sat a tall, pointed cap. He looked just like a wizard. He was dressed just like a wizard. And in fact that is what he was, a wizard.

"Don't be so stupid, boy. How can a pot be on fire? Pots can't burn when they're made of metal!" His voice was kind, but during the past few days he had begun to get a little tired of this boy. Perhaps he had been wrong to take him on as an apprentice, and yet the lad had looked keen and had seemed willing. Perhaps there was still time for him to improve.

"It *is* on fire, master," said the boy again. "Look at all the smoke." Snake-like coils of steam were by now rolling round their feet.

"Steam, boy, steam! Not smoke – *steam*! And don't worry

7

about it anyway, it's a special sort of wizard's steam which won't burn or hurt you in any way at all."

The boy still looked and felt doubtful. Since he had become apprenticed to the great wizard, Master Rudolfo, he had been burned and hurt more than once.

He remembered still the time he had stolen a very small cake from the wizard's tea-plate, only to find that as soon as he got outside, the cake had begun to shout "Help! Help! Someone is stealing me!" The stripes caused by the wizard's cane on his bottom were still there.

Then there had been the beautiful golden drink in a tall frosted glass standing by the wizard's bedside. The boy had only taken such a very small sip, but it had been enough to burn his tongue and leave a nasty blister. How was he to know that the drink was part of a spell that took fifty years to complete?

Master Rudolfo sniffed, and shuffled across the floor to the pot. He poked inside it with his long staff, stirred around and then lifted something out, dangling on the end of the staff. It looked like a purple frog. The wizard pushed his glasses farther up his nose, examined the frog and then let it drop back into the pot again with a plop. He sighed and turned to the boy.

"Did you read the spell properly this time, Simon?"

The apprentice nodded eagerly. "Oh yes, master." He pointed to a large book lying open on the cluttered bench.

"And are you sure you used the correct ingredients?"

"Oh, quite sure, master. That is ... er ... except for just one thing. The bottle of dried rosemary was empty so I used bat's blood instead. It was the same color and looked the same."

The wizard groaned. "Stupid boy! Will you never learn? The ingredients must be exact. Now, instead of making a very pleasant spell you have made a particularly nasty one."

"Nasty, master?"

"Yes, nasty! We should have had a good mutton broth bubbling away there, but you've managed to make instead a very horrid frog porridge. I've a good mind to make you sit down and eat it!"

Simon turned pale. He did not fancy frog porridge one little bit.

"Well, well, take the pot outside," said Rudolfo crossly, "and empty it on to the grass near the little stream. If the frogs happen to live, they might have purple tadpoles and that could be interesting. Go on, get on with it."

When he returned with the empty pot Simon found the wizard packing bottles and packets into a large black bag. The boy's face brightened. Perhaps they were going on a journey. He liked journeys. He remembered the last one when they had gone to cure the Duke's daughter of flat feet. He had enjoyed living in the palace for a week.

"Are we going away, master?"

"No, Simon, I am sorry but I cannot risk taking you with me this time. Not after what happened to the Duke's daughter's toe-nails because of your ... oh never mind, that's all in the past. But I hate to think what might happen to the Count of Corbello if I took you along to help get rid of the wart on his nose!" He laughed and cackled. "But I shall be back very soon. It's a job I can do very quickly when left in peace."

Simon was disappointed. "What shall I do while you are away, master?"

"Do nothing. That should suit you. Just try to keep out of mischief. Look after the house and tell any callers that I shall be back tomorrow. There are just two messages. If Mistress Baker calls for her love-potion, you can give her this bottle of pills. And if Farmer Hawkins comes round to collect the cure for his pigs' loss of appetite, then give him that powder. Is that quite clear?"

"Yes, master, bottle for Baker, powder for pigs."

"Well then, don't touch anything else. I shall be back at midday tomorrow. Have the giant cauldron full of water and boiling for me – I may need it."

"What, that one which holds as much as a bath, master?"

"Yes, boy, it will be good exercise for you to carry enough water to fill that! Now then, any questions before I go?"

"No, master. You can count on me."

"I can usually count on you to make a mess of things. However, I suppose if you are to become a wizard one day then I must try to leave you on your own sometimes. But don't touch anything, and don't meddle!"

The day passed slowly. Simon ate a large piece of red cheese and an onion for his midday meal, washed it down with a glass of water, and waited. Nothing happened. The house was very quiet.

Soon the boy noticed that the wizard had left out on the bench his large leather-bound book of spells. Usually it was locked carefully away, but this time, what with the purple frogs and the wizard's sudden departure, it must have been forgotten. There it was, temptingly open.

Simon went over and began turning the pages idly, reading the names of the spells. "How to walk on the ceiling". That would be useful. "How to become as small as a fly". That too would be useful, as long as he wasn't swatted as a result! He scanned the list of ingredients, some of which were very strange and whose instructions were written in a strange language. They would be no use to him.

At that moment there was a knock on the door and a blushing young woman asked if her love-potion was ready.

"Ah, yes," said Simon, trying to sound like his master. "Let me see now, the potion. Powder for potion, I think. Yes, that's right, powder for potion." He handed the girl the packet of powder and she went off giggling.

He had hardly settled down to the book again when

there came another knock at the door. This time it was Farmer Hawkins.

"Ah yes," said the boy. "Pigs with no appetites. Let me see now, it was pills for pigs." He handed over the bottle and the farmer clumped away.

Simon went back to the wizard's book of spells. "How to make a stool walk on its own legs". Not much point in that, he thought, unless of course you were tired and wanted to be taken around sitting on a stool. He laughed aloud at the thought.

Then at last he came across a spell that he thought might be very useful: "How to turn your broom into a willing servant".

Simon's gaze wandered round the cluttered room. There in the corner, leaning up against the wall, was a fine broom. Alongside was the huge pot-bellied cauldron which he had to fill with water in the morning. All the water would have to be carried in buckets from the well outside. Now, if he could only turn the broom into a willing servant, then the broom could do all the work while he sat on the stool and watched!

The more he thought about it, the more the idea appealed to him. Master Rudolfo would never know, because everything would be back to normal before he came home. He began to get excited and went back for another look at the spell, reading the words to himself from the stained and crinkly page:

> "Stand the broom upright, hold in the hand,
> Sprinkle the floor with a handful of sand.
> Touch broom with water and scale of a fish –
> It's now your servant to do as you wish.
> Be sure that you. . . ."

Simon did not bother to read any more. He went to bed that night delighted to think that the broom was going to do all his work for him in the morning.

11

Simon was awake and up early. He dragged the great cauldron across the floor, hoisted it on to the tripod over the fire, and then turned to the broom. He held it upright with trembling fingers. He cast a little dry sand on the floor, dipped his fingertips into a jar of water, and then touched the broom with them. Finally he reached into a little dish close by, took out a gleaming fish-scale and dabbed it on the broom handle.

As he did so the broom quivered under his fingers. Then it shook. Simon let out a yell and dropped it in fright. Before his astonished eyes two little arms sprouted out of the handle of the broom, a weird little head with a shock of red hair and a grin on its face appeared at the top, and small but sturdy feet grew from among the bristles.

The broom bowed to Simon, at which he fell over backwards and sat on the floor with a bump. The broom's face grinned even more and suddenly a squeaky voice said, "Yes, my lord, what can I do for you?"

Simon was amazed. He had not imagined that the spell would really work, and now that it had done so he felt tongue-tied. He swallowed hard. "Er ... oh ... er ... yes ... er ... let's see – in that bucket, fetch water from the well outside and pour it into the cauldron."

The broom bowed, trotted on its tiny legs over to the bucket, picked it up in its little hand and ran off up the steps.

In a few moments it was back again, the bucket brimming over with water. It emptied its load into the cauldron which hissed comfortably, turned round and went off up the steps again.

Simon could hardly believe his luck. He sat on the stool and began to whistle.

The broom appeared again. Hiss went the cauldron. Up the steps and out of the door went the broom and the empty bucket.

It came again. Splash, hiss and off.

And again. Splash, hiss and off.

Again. Splash, hiss and off.

The cauldron was nearly full. Two more trips would do it easily.

Splash, hiss and off.

"Next one's the last," Simon shouted after the broom.

"That's enough! That will do! We don't need any more! Hey! Stop!" For the broom had gone off up the stairs as if it were going for another bucketful.

And so it was! Splash! Hiss!

The cauldron was almost overflowing. Simon made a wild grab at the brush, but it was so strong that it just dragged him across the floor and up the first few steps. If he had not let go it might well have pulled him outside and thrown him down the well!

Next minute another bucket of water was hurled into the overflowing cauldron. Most of it cascaded down the sides on to the fire and put it out. Wet grey ashes smeared the floor round about.

Splash! Another bucketful was poured, and now the floor was really wet.

Splash! Simon was desperate now. Then suddenly he had an idea. He grabbed a small axe used for chopping firewood, and as the broom went past him he swung at it, chopping it neatly in two!

For a moment he thought he had won. But then to his horror he saw that both halves of the broom had now sprouted arms and legs, both had got a grinning red head and, worst of all, both had got a bucket! Like twins they went off up the steps, and like twins they came back down again with brimming buckets.

Splash! Splash!

Simon flew at them and whirled the axe again. For a minute there were just four pieces of broken broom – but then . . . four little brooms trotted off with four buckets.

Splash! Splash! Splash! Splash!

13

The floor was ankle-deep in water, and floating in the flood were books, bottles, feathers, the wizard's second-best cloak and a dead mouse. Simon howled with rage and flew at the four brooms with the axe yet again, whereupon eight little brooms with eight buckets set to work. At this, Simon fled, screaming in terror, up the steps and out of the knee-deep water. He reached the top step, just as the wizard, face as black as a cloud, came in from outside, stepping round the row of scurrying brooms.

Rudolfo took in the situation at a glance. He raised his staff and in a voice of thunder cried "Stop!"

At once everything stopped. There was complete silence but for the drip, drip, drip of water from the old black cauldron. Little waves slopped round the foot of the steps.

Rudolfo looked down at his cowering apprentice. "Well?" he said, "What have you got to say for yourself?"

Simon was about to make some sort of excuse, indeed his mouth was already open, when from outside the house they heard angry voices.

"Where is that dratted wizard?" came the rough voice of Farmer Hawkins. "Those wretched pills did no good at all for my pigs' indigestion. Instead they've made them go all stupid, rubbing round my legs like tame cats! Where is that idiot? Just let me get my hands on him!"

Then came a woman's voice. "You wait your turn. I want him first. That so-called love-potion has cured my husband's indigestion, so that now he goes out all day and every evening and I never see anything of him at all! Just let me get hold of that wretched wizard!"

It took a long time to sort things out and to clean things up, and Simon was pretty tired and miserable by the time it was all done. He would have been glad of a rest, but the wizard had shown him another use for a broom handle, and Simon did not feel like sitting down at all!

Story Two
The Hidden Story

King Rameses the Great, Pharaoh of Egypt, sat on his golden throne and frowned. His pale hands, resting on the curved arms, were restless and the long fingers drummed a nervous rhythm. Below him, in a crescent, knelt his courtiers, foreheads pressed to the black marble floor, palms sweating with fear. Nobody was ever easy in their minds when Rameses the Great frowned.

Suddenly the King spoke and his words hissed like sand-snakes: "Get up!"

One of the courtiers, a tall old man in a long robe, rose to his feet with a struggle and faced his king. He was afraid, but somehow he found the words he wanted. "It is difficult, my lord. The man is from Ethiopia. He is a wizard. He speaks another language and sometimes his words sound strange. We humble ones cannot truly understand what he wants, but you, lord, in your wisdom. . . ."

Rameses hissed again. "What you mean, man, is that you know very well what he wants but you dare not tell me! Well, send for him and let him speak to me. Why do I have to be surrounded by fools and cowards? Fetch him!"

The great bronze doors swung open and in strode a huge black man. His long robe was black, held round the waist by a broad black sash. His hair was short and grey and his gaze was proud. A faint smile flickered round his lips. As he came to the foot of the throne he bowed low and then raised a powerful arm in greeting.

16

"Lord of the Nile, greetings from my royal master, the King of Ethiopia!"

The Pharaoh grunted and pretended to yawn. "What does your master want? He must want something. He usually does."

The Ethiopian bowed again. "Your Highness, my master wants for nothing at all. But he has sent me to tell you that he has a greater magician in his land than any in Egypt. Thus says my master, the King of Ethiopia."

For a moment Rameses looked startled. This was something he had not expected to hear. Egyptian magicians were thought to be the best in the world, and he had never heard anyone suggest that they were not. He thought hard while he looked at the brawny Ethiopian. If they had got a better wizard than he had, then Egypt's good name throughout the world would suffer.

He thought hard but said nothing. He merely grunted and waved a sand-fly from his face.

The Ethiopian bowed yet again. "Your Highness, I have to tell you that I am that magician, and my King has sent me here to challenge you to find a better."

This time Rameses really was startled. "You!" he exclaimed. "You! Well, master magician, what is it that you can do that my own wizards cannot?"

The Ethiopian smiled and folded his arms. "No, lord, let your wizards show me their greatest feats of magic first. Then I will show them what they cannot do!"

Rameses bristled with anger. "My magicians can do anything!" he snarled. "Anything!"

The black man showed a row of very white teeth, then reached inside his black robe. He brought out a tightly rolled scroll, tied round with black cord and sealed with a thick blob of red wax. He held the scroll out to show the Pharaoh. "Can your wizards read this scroll?" he said.

Rameses snorted and laughed. "Of course."

"Can they, then, read what is written on the scroll without first unrolling it? Can they leave the cords untied and the seal unbroken and still read the words?"

Rameses frowned. "That would seem impossible." And then, as he saw a smile hovering round the Ethiopian's lips he turned red and shouted, "Of course they can do it! Egypt has the best wizards in the world. I will find one to read your scroll. Come back tomorrow at the same time."

The man went, and as soon as he had gone Rameses began to worry. He knew many great magicians, but the greatest of them all had never said that he could read what was written inside a scroll which was still rolled up. Angrily he got up from his throne and paced up and down on the black marble floor. With a wave of his hand he dismissed the courtiers, who went out mumbling to each other.

Not long afterwards the bronze doors opened again and the Pharaoh's son, Setna, came in. "Father," he said, "I have just been told of this insolent dog's challenge to you. Stop worrying. I know who can read that scroll!"

Rameses grasped him by the shoulders. "You do, my son? Who is it? Who is this great wizard?"

Setna smiled. "He is well known to you. He is your very own grandson – my son, Se-Osiris."

Rameses heard these words with amazement. "But he is only a small boy!"

"Boy he may be, Father, but this task he can and will do!"

And so the next day the Ethiopian once again came before Rameses. "Your magician is ready, great and mighty one?" he asked with a sneer, holding up the scroll.

Rameses clapped his hands. "He is ready, insolent one."

A small boy stepped shyly forward. Huge brown eyes shone in his dark face. He fastened these eyes on the scroll and began to speak in a thin, high voice. "I read, mighty Rameses. I read what is written in the scroll." He paused and his lips moved silently. Then he began again. "It tells

18

a story, my lord. It tells a story about a King of Ethiopia and a Pharaoh of Egypt, and of a battle between their magicians."

Rameses leant forward. "Go on, boy, go on!"

The thin voice droned on, and this was the story that Se-Osiris read while the court listened:

"Once upon a time, the King of Ethiopia, walking in his fine gardens, overheard three of his court magicians boasting of their powers. Each of them was saying that he was the finest wizard in the world. At last after much argument, one of them said, 'I could do what nobody here has ever dreamed would be possible. I could use my magic to bring the great Pharaoh of Egypt under my power! I could use my magic to fetch him from his palace to this one! I could use my magic to have him beaten soundly and then returned as swiftly as he came!'

"The King of Ethiopia had heard enough. He stepped forward out of his hiding-place. Facing the boastful wizard he said, 'You speak well. Let us see if you can do what you say. I have no reason to love the Pharaoh of Egypt. If you can really do what you say you can, then do it! And do it tonight!'

"For the rest of that day the magician worked with his hands in secret. Then at nightfall he produced a model of a royal litter, made entirely out of beeswax and with four golden-robed bearers. He placed the tiny model on the floor and began to move round it chanting a spell.

"The magician's words rose and fell. Those watching smelt hot wax and the air grew thick and breathless. A deadly silence fell, and it was as if thick wadding were pressed over their ears. Then before their gaze the floor seemed to become liquid, a dull, rumbling noise got louder and then, suddenly, with a clap of thunder, the model had gone!

"A murmer arose among those present, but the magician stilled it with a raised hand. 'Wait!' he commanded. 'And watch!'

19

"He pointed, and on the floor where the model had been there appeared a faint white mist which began to grow thicker. Gradually the mist was transformed into the figure of a man, kneeling on the floor with a bewildered look on his face. As the mist cleared everyone could see that the figure was that of the great Pharaoh of Egypt!

"At the wizard's signal three slaves, stripped to the waist, now stepped forward. They raised knotted whips. A smile grew on the face of the King of Ethiopia as he watched the helpless ruler of Egypt, his rival, beaten and whipped.

"At last the slaves stopped, the wizard raised his arms and with a hiss the Pharaoh disappeared. There on the floor, where the beating had taken place, standing among the coils of the slaves' whips, was the wax model of a litter!

"Back in his own palace the Pharaoh groaned and cursed. Doctors rubbed him with soothing oils. Slaves lowered him gently into a scented bath and then dried him on soft towels. Mountains of cushions were piled round him. But as he sat he ached, and as he ached he called on the gods for help. It was midday before he fell into a troubled sleep. And as he slept he dreamed. He dreamed of huge slaves with whips, and his head was plagued with crashes of thunder. But then suddenly, as he dreamed, he felt that he was in the presence of a fantastic being, a tall wreathed figure with the head of a river-bird instead of a human face. He knew this to be Thoth, god of wisdom and magic, and he knelt at the god's feet.

"He dreamed that he told the god his story, and that the god spoke in a high, chattering voice: 'I, Thoth, am angry that the Pharaoh has been beaten. Tonight the waxen litter will come again, but this time I shall be with you and we shall see what happens then!'

"So that night the Pharaoh sat in his palace, and the King of Ethiopia sat in his, rubbing his hands at the thought

20

of seeing his rival beaten again. The magician produced the waxen litter, made a magic sign with his hands and stood back to see what would happen.

"But, to his horror, the King of Ethiopia found himself seized by invisible hands, forced into the litter, and then whirled through the air. His head reeled, and seconds later he lay sprawling on a marble floor at the feet of his rival the Pharaoh of Egypt! He screamed as he saw slaves with whips coming towards him, and he lost consciousness as the first blows fell. But just before he passed out he thought he saw a tall pillar-like shape with a river-bird's head, and heard a voice, shrill and high, chattering with long peals of laughter.

"Thus the Pharaoh, with the help of Thoth, gained his revenge."

Se-Osiris, having finished reading, bowed to his grandfather and stepped back. The Ethiopian wizard, who had been standing in silent amazement listening to the childish voice, seemed to come to life again with a start. "Am I to be defeated by a mere child?" he yelled angrily. "Then take that!" So saying he hurled the tightly rolled scroll at the young boy.

As the scroll fell to the floor it changed miraculously into a black snake which hissed venomously and reared its flat head to strike at Se-Osiris. But the young wizard just smiled. Without moving he lifted a finger and pointed at the snake. Instantly it lowered its head and was seen now to be nothing more than a harmless worm wriggling its way towards the door.

Shouts of laughter and triumph came from the assembled Egyptians, but the Ethiopian was not finished yet. He threw back his grizzled head and from his gaping mouth came pouring a black evil-smelling cloud. The cloud wreathed swiftly towards the boy wizard as if it intended to roll all round him and swallow him up!

21

Again Se-Osiris stood his ground. Reaching out with his small hands he grabbed at the edge of the cloud and pulled it towards him. As it came he squeezed it between his palms, pulling and crushing it until at last the cloud was just a small, crumpled black ball. The boy tossed this small ball carelessly into a nearby brazier, and it had gone!

The Ethiopian magician was by now both furious and frightened. He opened his arms wide, spat out a stream of strange-sounding words, and, to the horror of the watchers, sent a sheet of white-hot flame gushing towards Rameses.

Rameses was paralyzed with fear, but he need not have worried. This time Se-Osiris did move, and swiftly. He stepped calmly between his grandfather and the tongue of flame, crossed his arms on his chest and faced the oncoming fire.

The flames seemed to roar round both the old man and the boy, but neither of them felt the heat. For a moment they were lost from sight, and then, slowly but surely, the white-hot fire-ball began to revolve and move back in the direction it had come from. The Ethiopian wizard saw his danger and screamed with fear, but it was too late. He could do nothing. He was consumed by his own fire!

There was one blinding white flash which seared the eyeballs of the Egyptians and then the ball of flame vanished, leaving the palace room dark and gloomy. Of the Ethiopian nothing remained but a small, smoking heap of ashes on the floor. A wisp of smoke curled upwards to the high ceiling and died. A door opened somewhere and the draught scattered the ashes for ever.

The battle was over. Se-Osiris, the young wizard of Egypt, had triumphed!

Story Three

The Strange Case of the Detective Wizard

One of the most famous wizards of all time was born in Wales and is known as Robin Ddu. There are many stories of how he used his powers for good, and this tale tells how he was able to solve a crime by using magic – or perhaps it was not magic. You can read it for yourself and make your own mind up.

In a large country house in North Wales lived a rich old man who kept a large number of servants to look after him. He had several gardeners to grow crops in the kitchen gardens, and to look after the flowers and trees in the pleasure gardens. He had stable-boys and a coachman so that his horses and carriages were always ready for use. Inside the house he had a large kitchen staff; cooks to prepare the food and scullery maids to scrape and wash the greasy pans and dishes. Then there were maidservants and footmen to look after the house and serve the food, and a butler and housekeeper to supervise everyone else and keep the accounts. Many people then lived in and around the big house, all of them ready to serve their master honestly and well.

All except one, that is! For one day, as the master of the house wandered through the long gallery which ran across the front of the building, he noticed that something was missing. The portraits of his father, grandfather and many other ancestors still hung on the dark walls. The swords, shields and armour carried by his forbears still gleamed over the oak doorways at either end of the gallery. The fine china and polished glassware still stood on red velvet in the display cases and on the mahogany shelves. But the great silver cup, the two-handled silver cup which had once stood on the captain's table aboard a stately Spanish galleon as it sailed with the Armada, had gone! It had vanished! On the sideboard where it had stood for years and years there was now only a faint ring of dust.

The master of the house was thunderstruck. Where could the cup have got to? He looked frantically around the gallery to see if by accident some servant had put it in the wrong place after cleaning it. But there was no sign of it at all. Without doubt the cup had gone!

There was only one explanation for its disappearance. The cup must have been stolen. The master strode angrily over to the carved wooden fireplace and pulled at a silken tassel. Far away down in the butler's pantry a bell jangled. The butler got up, took off his baize apron, put on his black coat and went upstairs to do his master's bidding. He listened quietly while the angry man told him all that had happened.

"So I shall have to see all the servants. You'd better get them all together now, Thomas, so that you and I can question them one by one. Tell them to gather in the front hall immediately."

Ten minutes later all was ready. The master went to the top of the stairs and looked at the faces turned up towards him, each the face of someone he had thought he could trust. But as he looked his heart sank. How could he ever find out which one of them had stolen the silver cup? Could it be old Gwilym, the head gardener? Yet surely it was impossible for a man who grew such beautiful flowers to think of stealing anything? What about young Jim the boot-boy? He could certainly do so, but then he would never have the nerve. And Gwen, the parlourmaid? She often dusted the cup, but even if she had stolen it she would certainly not know what to do with it!

The servants waited in silence. They knew already what had happened. Some looked worried, some defiant, some sad – but nobody looked guilty. The master cleared his throat.

"Er ... hm ... you all know why we are gathered here. It was my intention to question you all one by one ... er ... that is, Thomas and I were going to question you all...." His voice faded away in embarrassment.

Mrs Williams the cook pulled at her apron and said, "I'm quite sure, sir, that nobody here would dream of touching, let alone stealing, your beautiful things. I'm quite sure, sir...."

"We had some gypsies round last week, sir," said a young gardener's boy. "Mr Gwilym, he chased them off soon enough, but perhaps they stole it."

"Gypsies? Do you really think gypsies would get into this house without being seen? Where's your sense, lad!" The master spoke quite sharply, and old Gwilym pulled the lad's ear to keep him quiet.

Thomas spoke firmly. "Nobody gets into this house," he said, "except for the master, his family and friends, and us servants."

"Then it *must* be one of us," said the gardener's boy again, stepping forward in his excitement. "And I know who'll find out the truth. No, stop it, Mr Gwilym, that's hurting!" Old Gwilym was pulling his ear again, but the master stopped him and gestured the boy to go on.

"You must send for Robin Ddu, master," said the excited lad. "Robin Ddu will find the thief!"

Now everyone there had heard at some time or other of Robin Ddu and there was some muttering at the mention of his name. The housekeeper crossed herself and said that she personally did not hold with wizards and magic. The young maidservants looked frightened and began to whisper

26

among themselves. The young men smiled, however, and nudged each other in excitement.

The master knew as well as everyone else that Robin Ddu was supposed to possess magical powers. For a moment he stood rubbing his chin and looking thoughtful.

"Ah ... er ... hm ... yes, Robin Ddu, eh? Well, well, well, Robin Ddu! Now then, I never thought of calling in a wizard. What do you think, Thomas, eh?"

The butler looked doubtful. "This person, sir, Robin Ddu as they call him, has been known to cure cows of the cough – but as for finding a missing cup ... well ... I doubt whether his powers are good enough for that."

One or two others among the older servants seemed to agree with the butler, but strangely the master seemed taken with the idea of consulting Robin Ddu. He had long wanted to meet the so-called wizard and this seemed a good opportunity to do so. In any case he had no idea himself how to get the cup back, and anything was better than just doing nothing and letting the thief get away with it. He gave orders to the gardener's boy to saddle the small brown mare and to ride over the mountain to fetch Robin Ddu.

A few days later Robin Ddu arrived, riding a shaggy white pony, his straddled feet almost catching on the ground as he trotted up the drive to the big house. He was a tall, thin man with a brown face and twinkling eyes. His fingers were long and brown and a gold ring gleamed on one of them. A necklace of Celtic design hung round his neck. His long white hair fell down to his shoulders.

Robin talked for some time to the master of the house and then went upstairs to the long gallery. There he stood and looked solemnly at the ring of dust where the cup had once stood. Meanwhile the master watched with interest, waiting for the wizard to make some attempt to perform a magic spell. The man appeared to read his mind, for he turned suddenly and said, with a sort of half-smile, "No, master, no magic to solve this crime. Not up here, anyway. Perhaps a wee spot of magic down in the cellar."

"In the cellar? Do you think that's where the cup's been hidden?"

"I know no more than you, master. But let's get to work." He pulled out a tall, pointed hat from an old bag he was carrying and placed it on his silvery hair. "Now, will you get all the servants together, please?"

Robin Ddu stood at the top of the stairs looking down at the servants, just as the master of the house had done. "Now then," he said. "I see you all, and my bones tell me that one of you is the guilty one. Who is it?"

No answer.

"The master here says that, if the guilty one owns up, he will not have to suffer any punishment on the spot, but that he will be dismissed and sent away. Now who is it who stole the cup?"

Several people shuffled their feet but otherwise remained silent.

"Very well then, I shall have to use my wizard's powers to find the guilty one. And the master will, I hope, be very strict and hard when I find him – or her." A young housemaid burst into tears and said afterwards that this was because the wizard had looked straight at her with his piercing eyes. "It was just as if he could see right through me," she said.

Robin Ddu straightened his tall hat, rubbed his chin with his long fingers and looked thoughtful for a while. Then at last he said, "Since the villain refuses to confess, master, we must use the Crying Cockerel. Please have one of the gardeners bring into the house the beautiful cockerel that I saw pecking among the peas as I rode through your kitchen garden on the way here."

A gardener's boy was sent immediately to fetch the bird.

"Next, master, your cook must find me the biggest cooking-pot she has."

It was done in an instant.

"Now then," said the wizard, "I am going down into the cellar. Down there, out of the sight of your prying eyes, I shall put a spell on the cockerel, which will give him a certain power. Then I shall put him on a table with the cooking-pot upside-down over the top of him. Then ... then. ..." His voice dropped to a whisper as he looked round the faces of the servants, but it was a whisper which carried right into every corner of that vast entrance hall. "Then one by one each of you will go down into the cellar alone!"

Again the housemaid burst into a flood of tears.

"Down there in the darkness," went on Robin Ddu, "you will put your hands on the pot. If you are not guilty, nothing will happen and you will come out smiling. But when the thief goes down there, if he so much as lays one single finger on that pot the cockerel will know that he is guilty, and will crow loudly, as if he is saying 'Thief! Thief! Fetch the constable! The thief is here!' "

There was silence except for the sniffling of the tearful housemaid. Then the master and the wizard carried the pot and the cockerel through the little doorway leading down to the cellar. After a short time they came out again, and told the first in the line of servants to go down. This was the cook, and down the stairs she went smoothing her apron.

Silence. Then up the stairs came the cook and out into the light, smiling. So she was not the thief.

Next went the little housemaid – to get it over with before she had hysterics – and again nothing happened. She too came up smiling through her tears.

One by one the line of servants went down the stairs and came up again. Each time there was silence, and no sound of the cockerel. So, as the last one came out of the cellar, blinking into the light of the hallway, the master turned to Robin Ddu with a frown. "What's the meaning of all this, then, wizard?" he grumbled. "Has your so-called magic failed,

then? Or was the cup stolen by an outsider and not by one of my servants?"

"Patience, master," smiled the crafty wizard. "I asked each of you, while you were down in the cellar, to carry out the test by placing your hands on the pot. Now, show me your hands, all of you."

First the master held up his hands, and there on the palms were sooty marks, dirt from the pot.

The wizard turned to the waiting line of servants. "Everyone show their hands!" he ordered. Pair after pair of sooty palms were raised in the air, but then, there, at the very end of the line, appeared one pair of spotlessly clean hands!

"There's your thief!" cried the triumphant wizard, and the butler – yes, it was the butler whose hands were clean – was dragged forward.

"There's your thief," said the wizard again. "You see, all of you went down and touched the pot knowing that you were innocent. But this man, knowing that he was guilty, did not dare to touch the pot in case the cockerel called out his guilt! And so his hands stayed clean while the rest of you got soot on your palms. Now, master, you must do with him as you will, my work here is finished."

The butler fell on his knees and confessed his crime. A servant was sent out and soon returned, holding the missing silver cup, which the butler had hidden among the dishes in his pantry.

At this point the butler broke down and started begging for mercy, saying how gambling debts had forced him into theft. But the master refused to listen, and told him to pack his bags and leave the house for ever.

Then the master turned to Robin Ddu, paid him well for his trouble and gave him the fine cockerel into the bargain. "After all," he said, "nobody will want to go near that bird again now that he is bewitched, will they? They will be afraid that he will tell all their secrets!"

31

Robin Ddu said nothing, and the master went on: "But then perhaps the cockerel is just an ordinary bird and never was bewitched after all."

Robin Ddu still said nothing. The cockerel may have been bewitched or it may have been just an ordinary bird. Whatever it was, its new owner was far from ordinary; and besides, he was far too clever to say anything!

The Flying Horse

The Sultan of Shiraz was fat. He was very fat, very fat indeed. He was so fat that all the horses in his fine marble stables were sway-backed. In fact the time had come when he had got so fat that he could not ride any of them. This meant that he got no exercise, and since he got no exercise he became fatter and fatter and fatter.

"Oh for a horse strong enough to bear my weight," he said one day as he sat on the roof-top of his palace, wriggling his little pink toes as they stuck out from underneath the tent of his robe. "I would give half my kingdom for a really strong horse."

He raised his eyes to the blue sky, whereupon, to his amazement, what he had taken for a seagull began to grow bigger and bigger. He rubbed his eyes and looked again. Cries of amazement were by now coming from his courtiers, for there really seemed to be no doubt about it. The Sultan was *not* seeing things. There, coming out of the sky, was a man, face split by a huge grin, legs wide apart and straddling a magnificent stallion!

As the Sultan gaped, his fat lips slobbering, the horse spread its legs and landed gracefully on the roof-top. Its rider slid to the floor and it was then, only then, that the Sultan realised that the animal was not a real horse at all, but one made of polished mahogany and gleaming gold. The rich

33

red leather of the harness hung loosely, not on a living neck but on a finely carved wooden one!

"Your Highness," said the man, bowing low, "allow me to introduce myself. I am known far and wide as the Hindu, and this is my famous flying horse."

The Sultan waddled, gasped and heaved his weight over to the horse. He stroked it and fondled it, then put his arm round its neck and said, "I *must* have it. It would be strong enough to carry me. Name your price!"

The Hindu bowed again, rubbed his hands together and then went over to whisper in the Sultan's ear. But this did not have the effect that he had expected.

"What?" roared the fat ruler, in a voice so loud that the Hindu almost fell flat on his back. "What? Guards! Take this villain and put him in the nastiest, darkest dungeon in the palace." Then, as the protesting Hindu was led away: "He dared to say that the selling price of his horse was the hand of my daughter in marriage! That foul fiend! To my daughter!"

Now it happened that the Sultan's favourite son was standing close by. "Stop, Father," he said quietly. "Before you send him to the dungeon, get him to show me how the magic horse works. Otherwise we shall never be able to use it."

Craftily the Sultan turned back again to the frightened Hindu and waved the guards away. "Now, man," he said. "I might yet be interested in your offer. But my son, the Prince here, must test out the horse. Show him how it is ridden."

The Hindu stepped forward at once. "There is a wooden peg, Your Highness, just by the saddle. Sit in the saddle, turn the peg and it will take you wherever you wish to go...."

Immediately the young Prince leapt into the saddle, turned the peg and, to the astonishment of the onlookers, rose into the air on the horse's back and was gone like the wind!

"Wait! Wait, Your Highness!" bellowed the Hindu in terror. But it was too late, for the Prince and the horse were just a speck in the sky.

For quite a time the court waited for the young Prince to return. An hour passed, then two, then three. The day was wearing on. At last the Sultan turned to the Hindu, his fat cheeks wobbling with rage and worry.

"Where is my son, miscreant?"

The Hindu fell on his knees in terror. "He flew off so quickly, Your Majesty, that I had no time to tell him that one peg makes the horse go off, while there is another peg, hidden behind the horse's ear, that will make it come back again. If he doesn't find that second peg he will never be able to come back!"

"What?" screamed the Sultan. "Guards! The dungeon!" And the Hindu, who was really a wizard up to no good, was dragged off.

Meanwhile the rash young Prince had discovered his mistake. No matter which way he turned the wooden peg the horse flew on, away from the palace, away from his father and his people. They had flown over high, snow-capped mountain peaks, over blue seas and over deep forests before the Prince finally found the second key and twisted it.

Slowly, gracefully, the horse drifted downwards, through traces of cloud, down through the moonlight, until it finally landed on the roof-top of a magnificent palace, the home of the Princess of Bengal.

It was night-time and everyone in the palace was asleep. The Prince got off the horse's back, and crept silently down a flight of marble stairs until he suddenly found himself in the sleeping quarters of the Princess herself. There she lay, on a silken bed behind gauzy curtains, and as soon as he set eyes on her the Prince fell madly in love.

Creeping up to the side of the bed, he drew the curtains aside and laid a soft hand across the Princess's mouth. As

35

her startled eyes opened wide he spoke in a whisper, "Beautiful lady, don't be afraid. I am the Prince of Shiraz, carried here by magic. I mean you no harm, and only beg that you will give me leave to rest awhile before I tell you my wonderful story."

The Princess nodded, and clapped her hands for her servants. They were amazed to see a strange man in the palace, but before long the Prince was resting on a soft bed in a quiet room sleeping and dreaming of the beautiful Princess and of the wonderful horse.

It did not take the Prince and the Princess many days to get to know each other. Before long they had agreed to get married, and the Prince made swift arrangements to take his bride-to-be back to his own land, to see his father in Shiraz. And since he had arrived by magic horse, that is how they went back, sailing through the sky with the Princess clinging on behind the Prince and shouting aloud with excitement at the ride.

As his father's city came into sight, the Prince set the horse down in the grounds of the Summer Palace, a mile or so away from where his father lived. He settled the Princess in comfort there and then took a real horse from the stable and galloped off to break the news of his return.

What a fuss everybody made of him when he arrived at his father's court! The bells pealed and cheer after cheer rang out while the fat old Sultan's many cheeks wobbled with delight.

The Prince told his amazing story, but when he reached the part about leaving the Princess at the Summer Palace the Sultan clapped his hands.

"Bring me my state robes," he ordered. "For I must go to greet my future daughter-in-law." And then, as the servants hurried away, he added, "Oh, and let that evil Hindu wizard out of his dungeon. Tell him to take his wretched horse and go!"

Now the guard who went to let the Hindu out of prison happened to be a bit of a gossip, so he told the wizard all the latest news. The Hindu immediately saw that here was a way of getting his revenge on the Sultan for having shut him up for so long – and for no good reason. So, once out of his cell, he got on a horse and rode off like the wind to the Summer Palace. Dismounting at the gate he hammered on the mighty doors. "I come from the Sultan," he announced grandly. "You know me: I am the owner of the flying horse. It is the Sultan's wish that I take the Princess on the back of the magic horse to the Palace where her bridegroom awaits her."

The Princess was overjoyed, but as soon as they were both seated on the horse's wooden back, the Hindu twisted the peg, set his face away from Shiraz and took them winging upwards into the clouds and towards the far land of India!

Hours later they landed in a sunlit forest in the Kingdom of Kashmir.

"Stay here!" ordered the Hindu to the weeping Princess. "I am going to fetch food so that we can eat before you marry me."

However, it so happened that the King of Kashmir was hunting close by, and he heard the Princess sobbing and crying for help. "What are you doing to that woman, man?" he said as he and his friends rode up.

"Go away and mind your own business!" said the wizard in a rude voice. "She's my wife and I can do as I like!"

But the Princess threw herself at the King's feet and gasped out the true story. She was so beautiful and looked so truthful that the King of course believed her. "Scoundrel!" he said in a grim tone to the Hindu. "How dare you lay your evil hands on a real princess?" And he signalled to one of his huntsmen, who promptly put an end there and then to the Hindu's life by chopping his wicked head from his body.

37

Well, you may think that that must be the end of the story. But if so, you would be very wrong, for the Princess was still in Kashmir, and her Prince – her sad Prince – had disguised himself as a wandering holy man and had set off to travel the world in search of his lost bride.

If the King of Kashmir had been a good man, all would still have been well. But he was far from being a good man, and so he decided to keep the Princess and persuade her to become his wife. She was escorted to his fine palace and locked away while the preparations for a grand wedding feast were made.

The poor Princess thought that her troubles would never come to an end. However, she still had her spirit, and she cast about in her mind for a way to delay the wedding. Soon she hit on a marvellous idea. She would pretend to go mad, knowing full well that no man would want to marry a madwoman!

So when the King of Kashmir sent for his bride-to-be he was horrified to see her screeching and wailing and tearing her hair, while foam ran from her mouth.

"What!" he said. "Am I to marry a madwoman? It would be better to send her back to her father!" But then he rubbed his chin and said, "Madness is an illness, and all illnesses can be cured. A bag of gold to the doctor who makes my Princess sane again!"

Doctors came and doctors went, but still the beautiful Princess tore her hair and foamed at the mouth.

Then one day who should come into the town but a young holy man, travelling from Shiraz, and it was not long before he heard the gossip in the bazaar that the King had a beautiful but mad bride.

The Prince of Shiraz, for of course it was he, rushed off to the palace and offered to try to cure the Princess. Once alone with her he dropped his disguise and wept tears of joy at the reunion.

39

"But how can we escape?" said the Princess. "This King of Kashmir has ten guards outside my room and others all round the palace. I have already seen what they can do with their swords and I do not wish to lose my head."

But the Prince had a plan. He went to the King and bowed before him.

"Your Majesty," he said. "I believe the Princess is suffering from an enchantment put on her by the wicked Hindu."

"Go on," said the King.

"The cure, I believe, lies in the strange wooden horse which the Hindu had with him when he died. Is it close at hand?"

"Yes, most certainly. I had it put in the palace museum, since it appeared to be of no use."

"Then bring it into the courtyard tomorrow at midday and you shall see how the Princess will be cured by it."

The hot noon sun burned down on the courtyard the next day as the Princess, heavily veiled, was led out. Armed guards were everywhere and the King smiled as he sat on his carved chair. Out of an arched doorway came the young holy man, and he took the Princess over to the wooden horse. "Now, Your Majesty," he said to the King. "The Princess will climb into the saddle and you will see the cure begin."

The Princess seated herself, the disguised Prince leapt up behind her and reached for the wooden peg. Then to the astonishment of the court and to the fury of the King, the horse rose into the air and hovered over the courtyard. There it remained just long enough for the Prince to call down, "Great King, when you wish to marry a princess you should first of all make sure that she wishes to marry you!"

Then, settling themselves comfortably on the broad wooden back, the young couple flew swiftly off towards their home and safety.

How the Warlock Won a Wife

Nearly four hundred years ago in the little village of Saltpans there lived an old schoolmaster. His name was John Cunningham, but everyone knew him as Doctor Fian.

Doctor Fian did his teaching in the porch of the church at Saltpans. This was the custom at that time, for it was long before schools were built as special places of learning. Two or three boys, the sons of rich farmers and gentlemen, used to come every day to Doctor Fian to be taught how to read and write, and how to translate from Latin and Greek into English.

One of the schoolmaster's oldest pupils was a lad called Richard Seaton. Richard's father was well-to-do. He owned a large house and several farms. He was much respected by everyone around and he lived a happy family life. However, in spite of being one of the oldest pupils, Richard was not very clever. He had great difficulty in learning the names of the letters of the alphabet, he grasped his long quill pen as if it were a pitchfork, and his writing was crabbed and scratchy. As for Latin and Greek, he seemed to make no progress with them at all. He just could not understand what his teacher was trying to get him to do.

Day after day Richard went to the little school to learn his lessons, and day after day he returned home black and blue from the whippings Doctor Fian had given him. When he got home his father would also scold him for not learning, and his older sister Jean laughed and teased him for his stupidity.

The only person who worried about Richard was his mother. She did not like Doctor Fian; he had an ugly, twisted face and when he grinned, which he only seemed to do when hurting somebody, he showed broken yellow teeth between his thick lips. So Mrs Seaton was horrified, even a little frightened, when one day Doctor Fian stopped her as she walked in the village and begged leave to speak to her on an important matter. "What is it that you want?" she said, trying to get past him.

But the ugly schoolmaster blocked her way, lifted his black hat to her and bared his bad teeth. "Mistress," he replied, "your son Richard is a very poor scholar."

"So he should be, the way you beat him, Doctor Fian," said Mrs Seaton.

"It is a well-known fact that all boys learn a lot better when they are beaten every day, madam. I shall continue to beat your son every day until he stops being so stupid." Again the teeth were bared. "But it is not your son's stupidity that I wish to speak to you about."

"Well, then?"

"It is another matter."

"Then speak, man, I have no time to waste here with you." Mrs Seaton was getting angry.

The doctor cleared his throat and turned his battered hat almost nervously in his fingers. "You ... er ... also have an ... er ... that is, you have a daughter."

"Why yes, you know I have. Her name is Jean. What about her?"

"She's a ... er ... um ... a handsome girl, madam. Takes after her mother, no doubt." Here the doctor gave a slight bow.

"Well?"

"Well, it's like this, madam. I am not married." And now

42

the words all seemed to come out with a rush. "I am not married, but I am in need of a strong wife to keep me company, and to get me good meals, and to help me in my work. I was thinking perhaps that your daughter Jean would make me such a wife."

Mrs Seaton stepped backwards away from the schoolmaster. She could hardly believe that this wretched, ugly little man, older than herself, should be making her an offer of marriage for her beautiful daughter!

She found her voice at last. "How dare you!" she raged. "Never would I let her come anywhere near you, especially after the way I've seen you bullying my son. You, marry my daughter? I would sooner see her married to the toad that lives in our drain! Now kindly get out of my way – I have better things to do!"

The schoolmaster stood aside, bowing, then he replaced his old hat and shuffled off. As he went, Mrs Seaton could hear him muttering and cursing to himself. She crossed herself and went shakily on her way, angry still at the thought of what the horrid man had suggested.

Now, on the very next day, when Richard arrived for his daily lesson, he noticed a great change in the way Doctor Fian treated him. Instead of shouting at him and aiming blows at him, as had been the case in the past, the schoolmaster was kindly spoken and seemed full of praise. Richard could not understand it, for whatever he did seemed to please the old man.

However, at the end of the lesson he found the reason why. The schoolmaster caught him by the sleeve and took him outside the porch, whispering in his ear as he did so.

"Richard, you have been a very good boy today. You have worked well."

"Yes, master," said the surprised boy. "Thank you, master."

"You like it better when I praise you instead of beating you?"

"Oh yes, master, much better, thank you master."

"Then listen to me. Tomorrow I shall beat you very hard, very hard indeed. I have a nice new leather whip and I intend to use it on your lazy back. That is, unless. . . ." His grip on the lad's arm tightened so that the boy cried out in pain and fear. The man's dark eyes seemed to burn and he thrust his grizzled face close to the boy's. "Unless you do a very simple thing for me. All I want you to do is to bring me three hairs from your sister's head. Just three hairs from her head. Will you do it?"

"Three hairs, master?" stammered the bewildered boy. The grip on his arm was fierce and he winced with pain.

"Just three hairs from her head. That's all. Now, if you manage to do that for me, I promise that I shall never beat you again. Never. However, if you do not manage to do it, my new whip is just begging to be used, and it is thick and strong! Now then, what do you say?"

The schoolmaster gave Richard's arm a final wrench and then let him go. The boy began to weep, but seeing no way out he promised to do as Doctor Fian had asked him to. Instantly the evil man fetched out a piece of paper, covered with strange markings, and pressed it into the boy's hand.

"Tonight, then, while your dear sister is asleep, creep into her room and snip, snip, snip three hairs from her head. Wrap them carefully in this paper. Keep them safely and bring them to me at school in the morning. Do you understand?"

"Yes, master," said the trembling boy. "But why am I to do this strange thing?"

"Ask no questions. Just do it, and so make sure that you are never beaten again. Fail me and. . . ."

The threat was left unfinished, but Richard knew exactly what the doctor meant.

So that night, when the household were all asleep, Richard took his knife and padded softly in bare feet into the room where his sister lay asleep. Her dark hair lay in curls on the white pillow and she breathed easily and gently. Carefully the boy stole up to the bedside and reached out with his knife. Snip – one long hair lay in his hand. Snip – there lay another. Snip – but the third cut came just as the sleeping girl turned over in the bed. It jerked her hair and she awoke screeching with pain.

Poor Richard could do nothing but stand there in terror, while the rest of the family, holding candles, came running to see what was the matter. Then, as his father in a voice of thunder demanded to know why he had done such a thing, he gasped out the whole story.

"Show me the paper," said his mother, and Richard handed over the strangely marked paper which the doctor had given him to wrap the hairs in.

Mr and Mrs Seaton took one look at the paper and then began to cross themselves hurriedly.

"Witchcraft!" thundered Mr Seaton. "So all those stories of his being in league with the devil are probably true after all. I shall have him hanged for this. This is because you refused to let him marry our daughter, wife. This was the way he was going to get her anyway for his own evil ends!"

Richard and Jean were frightened and puzzled, so their mother did her best to explain. "It is a well known fact," she said, "that warlocks and their witch servants can make a person come to them if they can get hold of a hair from their head. It's a sure thing, that if Doctor Fian had managed to get hold of these precious hairs Jean would have found herself in his power, and bound to obey his wishes for ever and ever. She would have become his wife, and might even have been turned into a witch herself!"

"But what shall I do?" sobbed the frightened boy. "If I don't take him three hairs, Doctor Fian will beat me black and blue with his new whip."

"Don't worry about that. I have an idea," said Mrs Seaton.

"The evil doctor shall have his three hairs all right. But they won't be these three. I am going down to the cow-byre and I am going to pluck three long silky hairs from the tail of that young cow we have just bought. And then we shall see what we shall see!"

Down to school went Richard the next morning, taking with him the paper, inside which were three dark hairs, and pushed it into Doctor Fian's grasping hand. Without a word the schoolmaster scurried off into the church and soon the boys could hear his voice chanting strange-sounding words. Peering through a crack in the door Richard could see him crouched over the paper, holding one of the hairs in each hand. An evil smell hung in the air and all of a sudden it was very cold. Something was about to happen!

Suddenly from outside came a violent bellowing, and then to the astonishment of the group of watching boys, and to the dismay of the old schoolmaster, a young black cow came bursting into the church. It made straight for the schoolmaster, bellowing!

The doctor began to scramble to his feet, but the young cow rushed at him and butted him with her hard head, sending him flying and skidding across the church floor on his back.

Gibbering curses, the wicked doctor got to his feet and ran for his life, out of the porch and out of the churchyard into the village street. After him charged the cow, bellowing loudly, and neither of them stopped for a long, long time.

Doctor Fian came to a very bad end. Now that he had been found out, all sorts of people began to come forward with stories of how he and an evil band of witches had terrorised and put spells on them. Some time afterwards he was brought to court and tried for witchcraft. The judge found him guilty and he was executed for his wickedness. And all because he asked for a wife and got more than he bargained for!